W9-BJG-578

Peter's Painting

BY **SALLY MOSS**

ILLUSTRATED BY **MEREDITH THOMAS**

Peter painted a bird.
He painted it over and over.

And the more Peter painted,

the more his bird flew.

Peter's bird flew
and flew and flew.

5

Peter painted a snake.

He painted it over and over.

And the more Peter painted,

the more his snake slithered.

Peter's snake slithered
and slithered and slithered.

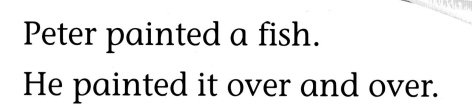

Peter painted a fish.

He painted it over and over.

And the more Peter painted,

the more his fish swam.

Peter's fish swam
and swam and swam.

Peter painted a star.

He painted it over and over.

And the more Peter painted,

the more his star twinkled.

Peter's star twinkled
and twinkled and twinkled.

Peter painted a door.

He painted it over and over.

And the more Peter painted,

the more his door opened.

Peter's door
opened
and
opened
and
opened.

21

And Peter leaped into the world,

into the world he had painted.